Ripley's Believe It or Not!®

Developed and produced by Ripley Publishing Ltd

This edition published and distributed by:

Mason Crest
370 Reed Road, Broomall, Pennsylvania 19008
www.masoncrest.com

Printed and bound in the United States of America.

First printing
9 8 7 6 5 4 3 2 1

Ripley's Believe It or Not!
Awesome Feats
ISBN-13: 978-1-4222-2562-2 (hardcover)
ISBN-13: 978-1-4222-9237-2 (e-book)
Ripley's Believe It or Not!—Complete 16 Title Series
ISBN-13: 978-1-4222-2560-8

Library of Congress Cataloging-in-Publication Data

Awesome feats.
     p. cm. – (Ripley's believe it or not!)
ISBN 978-1-4222-2562-2 (hardcover) – ISBN 978-1-4222-2560-8 (series hardcover) –
ISBN 978-1-4222-9237-2 (ebook)
1. Curiosities and wonders–Juvenile literature. 2. World records–Juvenile literature.
I. Title: Awesome feats.
 AG243.P67 2012
 031.02–dc23
                            2012020790

PUBLISHER'S NOTE
While every effort has been made to verify the accuracy of the entries in this book, the Publisher's cannot be held responsible for any errors contained in the work. They would be glad to receive any information from readers.

WARNING
Some of the stunts and activities in this book are undertaken by experts and should not be attempted by anyone without adequate training and supervision.

Ripley's — Believe It or Not!®

Disbelief and Shock!

AWESOME FEATS

www.MasonCrest.com

AWESOME FEATS

What unbelievable achievements. Be amazed at the

outrageous stunts, incredible skills, and awesome

performances inside this book. Read about the man

who rode a rollercoaster for 17 days, the woman

who has collected around 9,000 pieces of shoe

memorabilia, and the man who can pick up two

pails of water using his eyelids!

Tim Arfon's jet barstool racer can reach
speeds of 40 mph (64 km/h).

Foodscapes

Photographer Carl Warner creates beautiful, realistic landscapes with a secret ingredient—they're all made of food.

He makes forests from broccoli, clouds from cauliflower or mozzarella cheese, mountains from bread, and buildings from Parmesan cheese. What appears to be a natural view of a sunlit fishing boat at sea turns out to be a pea pod "boat" resting on a "sea" of smoked salmon, bordered by pebbles made from soda bread and potatoes, and a beach of brown sugar.

Carl from Kent, England, has been perfecting his amazing artworks—called "Foodscapes"—for the past few years. He says: "I begin by drawing a conventional landscape using classic compositional techniques, as I need to fool the viewer into thinking it is a real scene." He plans each image carefully, scouring supermarkets for ingredients. Finding the right shaped broccoli to use for a tree is crucial to his art.

With the help of model-makers, he then creates the set on a table top that measures 8 ft (2.4 m) wide. Each set takes up to three days to build and photograph. The various foodstuffs are either glued or pinned in place. Next, the scenes are photographed in separate layers, from foreground to background and sky, to stop the food wilting under the lights. Then the individual layers are put together on a computer to achieve the final image.

"My favorite scene has to be the broccoli forest," he says, "because it was the first one that went from my head to my sketch book to the finished image as a smooth process. It also raised the bar on how realistic I could make them look. It is the realization of what the real ingredients are that brings a smile, and for me that's the best part."

A smoked salmon and soda bread sunset scene looks good enough to eat.

This idyllic scene of a small village set in rolling countryside is made of dozens of different foodstuffs.

Ripley's research......

The snake handler can perform this remarkable stunt by making use of his nasal cavity—the large air-filled space above and behind the nose. He puts the snake into his mouth, closes his throat, and, with nowhere else to go, the snake is forced upward into the nasal cavity, from where it slides down his nostril and out of his body.

SWIMWEAR SHOOT

In September 2007, 1,010 bikini-clad women assembled at Australia's Bondi Beach for a huge magazine photoshoot.

UNDERSEA FLAG

On August 2, 2007, Russian divers planted the country's flag 14,000 ft (4,267 m) below the North Pole, on the bed of the Arctic Ocean.

UPSIDE DOWN

It's not enough for 17-year-old circus performer Erik Kloeker of Cincinnati, Ohio, to juggle sharp objects, eat fire, lie on a bed of nails, and swallow swords—he can even juggle upside down! In September 2007, wearing special gravity boots and hanging from scaffolding on top of the USS *Nightmare* at Newport, Ohio, he managed to juggle three balls upside down for over four minutes—a tremendous feat of abdominal strength, co-ordination, and concentration.

FLYING FEATHERS

A mass pillow fight lasting 30 minutes was staged outside the City Hall in Toronto, Ontario, Canada, in May 2007. The air was filled with feathers as about 200 people hit total strangers with down-filled pillows. Many participants dressed up for the event, wearing bandannas, ski goggles, and capes.

SHARP PRACTICE

At a May 2007 exposition in Moscow, a member of Russia's special police lay on a bed of broken glass and nails as knives were dropped point-first onto his chest!

MASS KISS

In August 2007, Budapest, Hungary, was the place to be for 7,451 happy couples who kissed simultaneously during a week-long music festival.

HEAD OVER HEELS

Don Claps of Brighton, Colorado, was head over heels with joy in 2007. He had just performed an incredible 1,293 cartwheels in just one hour on the TV show *Live with Regis and Kelly*.

SNAKES ALIVE!

A folk artist in Nanjing, China, can push a snake into his mouth and then pull it out through one of his nostrils!

SMASHING TIME

Yang Yuyin from China's Jiangsu Province can split bricks with one hand. His goal is to split 10,000 bricks in seven hours.

DR. SIZE

In 2006, Isaac Nesser lay down and lifted the front of a van off the ground! He had no idea how much it weighed, but says that the average car weighs 2,000 lb (900 kg). Nesser, of Scottdale, Pennyslvania, has been lifting weights since he was nine, and his muscular physique—weight 362 lb (164 kg), chest 74½ in (189 cm), neck 23½ in (60 cm), biceps 29 in (74 cm), and forearms 22 in (56 cm)—have earned him the nickname Dr. Size.

GALLAGHER GLUT

A total of 1,488 people with the surname Gallagher turned up at Letterkenny, County Donegal, Ireland, in September 2007 for the Global Clan Gathering. The Gallaghers had traveled from Ireland and Britain, and also from New Zealand and the United States.

PULLING PASTOR

The power of prayer helped Reverend Kevin Fast of Cobourg, Ontario, Canada, to pull two firetrucks, weighing a total of 69 tons, more than 98 ft (30 m). He achieved this in 1 minute 15 seconds, but needed two attempts, his first having been halted by a pothole near the finish line.

WRAPPED UP

New Zealander Alastair Galpin believes in keeping out the cold. In Auckland in 2006, he wore no fewer than 74 socks on one foot. On previous occasions he has worn seven gloves on one hand and 120 T-shirts!

DOLLAR CHAIN

On September 24, 2006, residents of St. Michael, Barbados, created a line of dollar coins that measured 1 mi 380 ft (1.73 km) long—adding up to more than $67,000!

BIG FOOT

In November 2007, the Sony Centre for the Performing Arts, in Toronto, Ontario, Canada, unveiled a stocking that measured 90 ft 1 in (27.5 m) long and 37 ft 1 in (11.3 m) wide from heel to toe.

APPLE PICKER

Fifty-year-old Claude Breton picked 30,240 apples, a total weight of 805 lb (365 kg), in eight hours in September 2007 at the orchard in Dunham, Quebec, Canada, where he works. Apple picking has been his passion for more than 30 years, and even when he works in a different job, he still spends his vacation picking apples.

SNAKE CHARMER

Snake man Jackie Bibby spent 45 minutes in a dry, see-through tub with 87 venomous rattlesnakes at Dublin, Texas, in 2007. Although the reptiles slithered all over him, none bit him. Bibby said afterward: "The key to them not biting is for me to stay still."

STRONG EYELIDS

Everyone else needs both hands to pick up two pails of water—but Li Chuanyong of Guangxi, China, can lift them with just his eyelids! He previously used his mighty eyelids to pull a car 16½ ft (5 m) along a road.

DARING STUNT
U.S. daredevil performer Brad Byers from Moscow, Idaho, can place a deadly tarantula or scorpion in his mouth and blow soap bubbles at the same time.

METAL MAN
Believing that the metal would cure his abdominal pains and create pressure to induce bowel movements, 30-year-old Pradeep Hode from Diva, India, swallowed 117 coins over the course of a few months in 2007. Sadly, Hode's plan didn't work and he had to have surgery to remove the coins.

BULB SWALLOWER
Harry Rifas, a former paratrooper from Bronx, New York City, could swallow seven flashlight bulbs and then bring them up again.

GLASS-EATER
An Indian fisherman eats crushed glass as part of his regular diet. Dashrath, known to residents of Kanpur as the "Glass Man," enjoys glass bulbs and bottles with his dinner and also eats lead bullets. He says that he's never had any health trouble and doesn't believe that the glass or bullets are causing him any ill effects.

IRON JAWS
Cai Dongsheng of Chongqing City, China, can snap nails with his jaws. He demonstrated his strength in 2007 by clamping four nails in a vice, wrapping them with gauze to protect his mouth, and then gripping the nails fiercely between his teeth. In just two minutes he had broken the nails.

MULTI-TASKER
Ray Steele of Alva, Oklahoma, could whistle with his tongue sticking out—and chew gum at the same time!

Turning Tomato

Nicholas Huenefeld calls himself "The Human Ketchup Drinking Machine"—and with good cause. His personal bests are quaffing 13 fl oz (384 ml) of ketchup in just 33 seconds—or 46 fl oz (1.36 l) of the red stuff in six minutes!

" In Huenefeld's own words...
I started drinking ketchup after a $5 bet at a local restaurant. I drank the whole bottle at the table and found it to be no problem. Drinking ketchup doesn't really affect me, unless I drink massive amounts. The only time I was affected was after drinking 46 fl oz (1.36 l). It took me a weekend to recover and not feel bloated anymore. I am currently training to increase my metabolism, which will help me breathe quicker and drink more quickly and intensely. One of my goals is to simply hold every ketchup record there is and be known as the world's greatest ketchup drinker. **"**

STEELY BITE

A performer takes a big bite out of a stainless-steel saucepan lid during festivities to mark the Chinese New Year in Beijing in February 2007. His tough teeth managed to bite the lid in two.

HARD TO SWALLOW

A huge tank filled with more than 80 sharks and stingrays was the watery setting for for a startling performance by world-renowned sword-swallower Dan Meyer, aka "Captain Cutless." Meyer, from Nashville, Tennessee, made history by becoming the first person in North America to swallow a sword while submerged 15 ft (4.5 m) underwater at Ripley's Aquarium in Myrtle Beach, South Carolina. He successfully swallowed a 24-in (61-cm) solid steel sword in a feat made many times more dangerous by being underwater and surrounded by large fish.

HOT STUFF

Manuel Quiroz, a 54-year-old taxi driver from Mexico City, Mexico, can eat dozens of spicy chili peppers, as well as rub them on his skin, and even squeeze their juice into his eyes—without feeling any discomfort at all. Quiroz first discovered his awesome talent when he was just seven years old. "Chilies don't sting me," he says. "They have no effect. It's just like eating fruit."

BALL JUGGLER

Francisco Tebar Honrubia, alias Paco, a Spanish entertainer who has performed with New York's Big Apple Circus, can juggle five ping-pong balls—using only his mouth and sending them up to 50 ft (15 m) in the air. He says the secret of his art is not to let his mouth get too dry.

TRICK SHOT

While blindfolded, Larry Grindinger of Duluth, Georgia, spat a cue ball out of his mouth onto a 9-ft (2.7-m) pool table so that the ball bounced over five rows of balls and sank four balls in two pockets.

MUSICAL TONGUE

Adrian Wigley from the West Midlands, England, played an organ nonstop for two hours— but he didn't use his fingers. Instead, he used only his tongue to hit the keys.

MOUTH PORTRAIT

In Chennai, India, in 2006, R. Rajendran painted a portrait of the then Indian President A.P.J. Abdul Kalam using only his mouth—it took him 127 hours. He produced this amazing piece of art by holding the brush with his tongue.

FOUR BALLS

Sam Simpson of Avalon, California, could hold either a baseball or three billiard balls in his mouth all at the same time—a feat he demonstrated at the 1933 World's Fair in Chicago, Illinois.

GIANT CROSSWORD

A self-confessed crossword fanatic from Yemen has created a giant crossword puzzle that is 178 times bigger than any other. Abdul-Karim Qasem spent seven years devising a crossword with 320,500 squares and 800,720 words in its accompanying clue book. He spent hours on end surfing the Internet to find information for his clues and answers, taking great care not to repeat any information in the puzzle.

11

CHINESE ACROBATS

Su Chuandong, a 63-year-old folk artist, from Wuhan, China, is able to float in a river while spitting fire. A former acrobat and lifeguard, he can also smoke, read a newspaper, and play the bugle while floating on the water.

SIMULTANEOUS SKIPPING
More than 3,000 people, ranging in age from ten to 68, assembled in the center of Changsha, China, in July 2007 to take part in three minutes of simultaneous skipping.

TOUR DE FAT
More than 3,600 cyclists, some riding homemade contraptions, took to the streets of Fort Collins, Colorado, in September 2007 for the Tour de Fat—an initiative aimed at promoting cycling as an alternative to driving. Many donned fancy-dress costumes, ranging from Miss Piggy to Fred Flintstone.

TRAM PULLER
In May 2007, Hungarian strong man Arpad Nick dragged a 70-ton tram more than 160 ft (49 m) through the streets of Budapest.

KING TOOTH
A Malaysian strong man nicknamed King Tooth pulled a seven-coach train using a steel rope clenched in his teeth. Rathakrishnan Velu hauled the 325-ton train 9 ft (2.8 m) along the track at Kuala Lumpur railway station in August 2007.

UNDERWATER HOOPER
Ashrita Furman of Jamaica, New York, hula hooped underwater for 2 minutes 20 seconds at a dolphin center in Key Largo, Florida, in 2007. While Furman was executing the stunt with a specially made metal hoop and breathing air from a portable scuba tank, the resident dolphins watched intently. "I think the dolphins thought I was totally crazy," said Furman afterward. "Who knows, maybe they'll try it themselves!"

PLANE DRAG
Using only his ears, Manjit Singh, 57, from Leicester, England, pulled a 16,315-lb (7,400-kg) passenger jet aircraft 12 ft (3.6 m) along the runway of East Midlands Airport in 2007. Prior to this event, his feats of strength included pulling a double-decker bus using only his hair and lifting 187 lb (85 kg) with only his ears.

STRONG EARS
Wang Lianhai from Qiqihaer, China, pulled a car for more than 650 ft (200 m) with his ears—but he was also riding a motorbike at the time! With his ears attached to metal clamps, which in turn were connected to steel wires, he pulled the $1\frac{1}{4}$-ton car, complete with its driver, along a street in Beijing in January 2007.

FITNESS FANATIC!

No wonder the people of Xi'an, China, flock to see this man showing off his flexible body during morning exercise—he's 75 years old!

ONE-HAND WONDERS ▼

328 coins	Dean Gould, Felixstowe, England, 1993
205 beakers on 41 trays	Abul Hashani, London, England, 1986
25 tennis balls	Julius B. Shuster, Jeannette, Pennsylvania, 1931
23 clothes pegs	Alastair Galpin, Auckland, New Zealand, 2006
23 cups	Blanche Lowe, Tyler, Texas, 1940
20 baseballs	Julius B. Shuster, Jeannette, Pennsylvania, 1931
7 full milk bottles	Joe E. Wiedenmayer, Bloomfield, New Jersey, 1932

EGG-STRAORDINARY!

Guo Huochun from Zhejiang, China, can pick up and hold 12 eggs simultaneously in one hand—without any of them cracking.

FREE THROWS

In August 2007, basketball-crazy Mike Campbell of Denver, Colorado, made 1,338 free throws in an hour—that's faster than one throw every three seconds. Throughout the 60 minutes he maintained a success rate of more than 90 per cent.

GO SLOW

Greg Billingham from Cheshire, England, deliberately ran the 2007 London Marathon in slow motion! Running one step every five or six seconds, he finished seven days after the rest of the runners.

NASAL POWER

A Chinese man pulled a $1\frac{2}{3}$-ton van and its driver more than 40 ft (12 m) with his nose. Fu Yingjie sucked one end of a thin rope through his right nostril and into his stomach, where he used his abdominal muscles to grip the rope and drag the van.

LOUD CLAP

A man in China can clap his hands almost as loud as the sound of whirring helicopter blades. Seventy-year-old Zhang Quan, of Chongqing City, has had his claps measured at 107 decibels—just three decibels lower than the sound made by a helicopter. Zhang does not clap very often, however, because the noise is so great that it hurts his ears.

HUG-A-THON

Utah college student Jordan Pearce hugged 765 people in just 30 minutes in 2007. However, the challenge was not all tender-hearted cuddles for the 18-year-old—a boy kicked and screamed to avoid being hugged by her, a man spilled his drink on her, and one girl refused to let go of her.

HAIR-RAISING

To celebrate India's 60th Independence Day in 2007, Siba Prasad Mallick of Balasore, pulled two motorcycles for a distance of 1¼ mi (2 km)—with his mustache. He began growing his 2-ft-long (60-cm) mustache seven years ago and keeps it strong by moisturizing it with mustard oil.

TREE-PLANTING

Farmers, students, and forestry officials in Uttar Pradesh, India, planted more than 10 million trees in one day on June 31, 2007!

She's Got Sole!

Darlene Flynn has certainly taken a shine to shoes. Since starting her collection in 2000, Darlene of Romoland, California, has accumulated around 9,000 shoe-related items.

She has at least 500 different kinds of shoe memorabilia—among them shoe-shaped furniture, shoe curtains, shoe wallpaper, shoe lamps, shoe watches, shoe-themed art, shoe teapots, shoe soap, shoe purses, shoe thimbles, shoe spoons, shoe candles, shoe salt and pepper shakers, shoe-styled stationery, an electric shoe toothbrush, and a red stiletto shoe phone. Darlene's house is lined with display cases of beautiful miniature shoes. She has some 7,000 in total, including one named Ms. Vicky that is just 4 in (10 cm) wide and cost her $1,800.

Outside, a cowboy-boot birdhouse hangs from the wall and the patio is decorated with shoe-shaped flowerpots. Her collection also includes a replica of the Disney Cinderella glass slipper, Barbie shoes galore, and a shoe made from ash collected from the eruption of Mount St. Helens. She has ambition to own a shoe-shaped car. Darlene started her collection after visiting her cousin's house for a Halloween party. "My cousin inherited her grandmother's shoe collection and when I saw it, I knew that was something I had to do. I don't know why it had to be shoes—I just love them and the whole thing kind of got out of control."

She has about 200 pairs that she wears herself, but one of her favorite items was made by her son for Christmas 2006. He spent over 40 hours gluing together coins totalling $15.07 into the shape of a shoe. For Darlene Flynn, it was the perfect present.

"In 2006, I had a special dinner event with Raine and other shoe collectors at my home in California. Everything was shoes, shoes, shoes—we had Cinderella shoe bottle-openers, shoe silverware holders, and so on, and the big finale was the shoe dessert. It took me between six and eight months to figure something out that would be completely edible."

"These are mainly my shoe thimbles—they are all approximately an inch high."

"This curio cabinet contains some of my signed 'Just the Right Shoe' resin miniature shoe collection. 'Just the Right Shoes' were the first shoes I bought for my collection. I am ecstatic about the release of my own 'JTRS' exclusive this year—'Graffiti Gurl Black.' These shoes are so popular because of the intricate detail and creative fantasy that Raine (the artist) puts into these little treasures."

"Most of the shoes pictured here are vintage or antique shoes. I received some as gifts but mostly purchased them myself while traveling around the U.S.A. and Europe."

"My shoe pin collection is quite unique. I have a wall hanging measuring 5 x 6 ft (1.5 x 2 m) that is covered with approximately 600 shoe and boot pins. Among my favorites are the Hard Rock Cafe shoe pins, my shoe breast cancer pins, and the boot pins."

DRILL SWALLOWER

In Cologne, Germany, in 2007, Britain's Thomas Blackthorne had a powerful jackhammer—a drill normally used for breaking up roads—lowered 10 in (25 cm) down his gullet and turned on for five seconds—and he survived. Blackthorne said his greatest fear was that the pneumatic drill would get stuck in his throat or knock all his teeth out!

TORNADO TERROR

Caught in a tornado-like storm in New South Wales, Australia, in February 2007, German paraglider Ewa Wisnierska was sucked up in a tornado tunnel to a height of 32,600 ft (9,946 m)—higher than Mount Everest. She ascended at a rate of 65 ft (20 m) per second, causing her to lose consciousness, and in an 80-minute ordeal she survived lightning, a battering from hailstones the size of tennis balls, temperatures as low as −50°F (−45°C), and a lack of oxygen. She reagained consciousness after 45 minutes and eventually managed to come back down to earth 40 mi (64 km) away, covered in ice and gasping for air.

MATH PRODIGY

In August 2007, Hong Kong Baptist University accepted math prodigy March Tian Boedihardjo as a student—at the age of nine.

PARROT FASHION

A four-year-old autistic boy, who has severe learning difficulties and could not speak, learned his first words thanks to his pet parrot. After listening to Barney the macaw, Dylan Hargreaves of Lancashire, England, mimicked the bird's vocabulary.

CARD ACE

Ben Pridmore of Derby, England, can memorize a shuffled deck of 52 playing cards and then recall them in the correct order in less than 30 seconds.

PI PATIENCE

In 2006, Akira Haraguchi of Mobara, Japan, recited pi to 100,000 decimal places from memory. It took him more than 16 hours.

BIRD TALK

Gautam Sapkota of Nepal can talk to wild crows and make them obey simple commands. He says he can utter 13 different crow calls and get the birds to respond. A keen bird-watcher for three years, he can mimic perfectly the calls of 115 species.

BLIND MECHANIC

Despite losing his vision five years ago in an auto accident, Larry Woody has continued to work as a mechanic in Cottage Grove, Oregon. He operates by feel, and to prove that disabilities need not be a handicap, he has recently taken on a deaf assistant.

MARY POPPINS

Blown off a six-story building in Zhejiang Province, China, by a sudden gust of wind in May 2007, schoolgirl Zhang Haijing landed softly after her open umbrella slowed her fall.

LUCKY CRASH

Bryan Rocco from Vineland, New Jersey, saved his own life by crashing his car into a tree. Choking on an onion ring while driving, he blacked out and smashed into the tree. Luckily for Bryan, the impact of the car hitting the tree dislodged the food from his throat so that he could breathe again.

FELLED BEAR

In 2007, a man killed a 300-lb (135-kg) black bear that was threatening his family—by throwing a log at it. Chris Everhart felled the bear with a single blow after it raided the family's campsite in the Chattahoochee National Forest in Georgia.

HUMAN HIBERNATION

A man survived for more than three weeks in a Japanese mountain forest without food or water in the first known case of a human going into hibernation. After breaking his pelvis in a fall, Mitsutaka Uchikoshi fell asleep and when found 24 days later, his body temperature had dropped to just 71.6°F (22°C). He was also suffering from multiple organ failure and his pulse was barely detectable. Doctors believe that after he lost consciousness, his body's natural survival instincts sent him into a hibernation-like state whereby many of his organs slowed while his brain remained protected. He made a full recovery.

FLAG EXPERT

A three-year-old Indian boy can identify the names of 167 countries from their flag colors. Aazer Hussain of Bangalore learned the flags in just 11 days after his parents bought him a poster of flags of the world.

HUMAN FLAG

Canadian gymnast and acrobat Dominic Lacasse can hold himself horizontally on a bar as a "Human Flag" for 39 seconds—a feat of incredible strength.

SELF-AMPUTATION

After being pinned under a fallen tree for 11 hours, 66-year-old Al Hill of Iowa Hill, California, freed himself by using a pocket knife to amputate his own leg.

CUSHIONED FALL

A woman in Nanjing, China, survived a six-story fall in April 2007 after her landing was cushioned by a pile of human excrement. She slipped from a balcony and landed in 8 in (20 cm) of waste, which workers on the street below had just removed from the building's septic tank.

Ripley's Believe It or Not!

Light Lunch

Wang Gongfu, of Lianyungang, China, eats glass twice a week. He ate his first glass cup when he was 20 and in the intervening 22 years he has eaten more than 440 lb (200 kg) of glass. His favorite is teacup glass, but he is also quite partial to electric lightbulbs.

Ripley's research

The risks associated with eating and swallowing glass depend on its size, shape, and sharpness, jagged pieces being far more dangerous than smooth. The human digestive tract can cope with many things—including bones in meat or fish—so small pieces of glass can travel right through the bowel and be passed out normally.

Sword swallowers must first eliminate the gag reflex, which they do by putting their fingers, then spoons, knitting needles, and eventually wire coat hangers down their throat. They must also relax their pharynx, esophagus, and the muscles of their neck, and make sure that the sword is lined up perfectly. Another trick of the trade is to lubricate the sword beforehand with either saliva or butter.

BALLOON JOURNEY

Five-year-old Kelvin Bielunski released a helium balloon from his school in Woodston, England—and three weeks later it was found by a soldier in Iraq, 2,500 mi (4,000 km) away!

WET CEREMONY

Taiwan's College of Marine Sciences staged its 2007 degree ceremony underwater! At the ceremony, which was held in the aquarium of the National Museum of Marine Biology, the university president wore a diving suit and handed out waterproof certificates to students whose graduation clothes were accessorized with flippers and oxygen masks.

HORSE SHOW

As a special attraction at the 2006 Stockholm International Horse Show in Sweden, Oliver Garcia of France rode his horse inside a massive plastic ball.

4,000 TRACTORS

In Cooley, County Louth, Ireland, in 2007, a total of 4,572 vintage tractors plowed a field simultaneously. All of the tractors involved were built before 1977, the oldest dating back 100 years. Farmers traveled from as far away as South Africa, Australia, the United States, and Canada to take part.

IT'S THE PITS!

Breathing air provided by algae watered with urine, an Australian marine biologist lived for 13 days in an underwater steel capsule 10 ft (3 m) long submerged in a flooded gravel pit. Lloyd Godson's survival at a depth of 15 ft (4.5 m) depended on a coil of green algae, which provided air in return for him urinating on the plants each day. Meals came in through a manhole in the capsule and he rode a bicycle to generate electricity, which recharged his waterproof laptop computer.

NASAL DRINKER!

A drink is not to be sniffed at for this performer in Hefei, China, in May 2007. He can drink the liquid by inhaling it through his nose!

STEEL SWALLOWER

This Chinese performer can swallow a stack of steel bars—without suffering any adverse effects.

ONTARIO SUPERMAN

For five minutes, Rick Ellis of Chatham-Kent, Ontario, Canada, hung suspended in midair from a piece of wood by eight steel hooks that had been inserted into his skin. The hooks—six in his back and one in each calf—had made the 36-year-old scream in agony as they were sunk into his skin, but once suspended he felt fine: "I wasn't in any pain then," he said. "I was at peace with myself. There was a lightness like there was nothing around me. It was like I was flying."

AQUA GOLF

A marine life aquarium in Fuzhou, China, staged what is thought to be the world's first underwater golf tournament. Five players overcame problems presented by fish, mammals, buoyancy, and water currents to play golf in a tank that was 50 ft (15 m) deep. The result was decided on how long it took to complete the hole rather than the number of strokes taken. The winner sunk the ball in 1 minute 20 seconds.

RAPID ESCAPE

Tied with chains and thrown underwater, Akash, a magician from Hyderabad, India, managed to escape from his shackles in a mere 15 seconds!

WET HAIR

Jurijus Levčenkovas of Vilnius, Lithuania, performed an underwater haircut in six minutes at an aquarium in July 2006.

BARREL ORDEAL

Apart from the occasional toilet break, Dutch philosopher Eric Hoekstra spent an entire week in April 2007 living in a 6-ft (2-m) wine barrel at Leeuwarden University.

STRONGMAN STUART

Stuart Burrell of Essex, England, lifted a 48½-lb (22-kg) weight 522 times in one hour!

ROUND OF APPLAUSE

Paramjit Singh of India, can clap his hands more than 11,600 times in just one hour!

BRA BUSTER

Thomas Vogel of Germany can unhook 56 women's brassieres in just one minute—using only one hand!

QUICK ESCAPE

An officer in the U.S. Navy took just 20 seconds to escape from a straitjacket—that's less time than it takes for a garage door to open and close. Performing as "Danger Nate" and wearing star-spangled running tights, Jonathan Edmiston freed himself from the regulation straitjacket at Yokosuka Naval Base's 2007 Fourth of July celebration.

KEYBOARD MARATHON

A Hollywood actor put himself in the spotlight in 2007 by continuously typing on a computer keyboard for five consecutive days (with a five-minute bathroom break per hour) in the front window of a Manhattan business center. Norman Perez said he stayed awake by chatting with strangers online and even received a marriage proposal.

THE HUMAN SLINKY

Romanian circus gymnast Ioan-Veniamin Oprea is able to contort his body into all manner of weird and wonderful shapes inside a colored plastic tube. With the aid of an assistant, he can even create a stunning octopus dance routine.

Oprea and his assistant in the slinky.

NOSE BLOW

Not content with blowing up a hot-water bottle with his mouth, 52-year-old Zhang Zhenghui, of Liling, China, has done it with his nose! After three years of practice, it took him just two minutes to blow up the bottle and make it burst. He has also used his nose to inflate the inner tube of a truck tire in only ten minutes, defeating competition from two young men with bicycle pumps!

WRITE ON!

Subhash Chandra Agrawal and his wife Madhu, from New Delhi, India, are never lost for words. Between them they have had more than 18,000 "letters to the editor" published in newspapers and magazines.

CHECK MATES

On October 23, 2006, 13,446 people gathered to play chess simultaneously in Mexico City's Zocalo Square.

Oprea's colorful plastic tube.

BACKWARD RACE
On August 20, 2006, a 7-mi (11-km) backward running race was held on the slopes of the Stanserhorn mountain in the Swiss Alps.

LONG SPEECH
Never pausing for more than 30 seconds at a time, India's Jayasimha Ravirala delivered a speech that lasted for 111 hours. His lecture on Personality Development Concepts ran for six days and five nights.

BRIDGE HOP
Six hundred people bouncing along on children's Spacehopper toys took part in a simultaneous hop on London's Millennium Bridge in April 2007. The bridge was chosen for the challenge because it wobbled alarmingly when it was first opened to the public in 2000.

LIQUID LUNCH
Five hundred people sampled a lavish dinner party in September 2007—underwater. The feast took place at the bottom of a swimming pool in London, England, but because of the difficulties of eating underwater, each of the three courses consisted of just one mouthful of food.

GLASS ROOM
Ye Fu and Hairong Tiantian lived in a single glass room on a sidewalk in Beijing, China, for a whole month. They were separated by a transparent wall in what they say is a metaphor for the gap in modern family relationships in China.

UNDERWATER HOCKEY
Eight international teams braved the freezing temperatures of an Austrian lake in February 2007 to take part in the first-ever World Underwater Ice-Hockey Championship. Competing under 12 in (30 cm) of ice, the players, wearing wetsuits, masks, and flippers, chased a Styrofoam puck around a "rink" that was 20 ft (6 m) wide and 26 ft (8 m) long. As they had no oxygen tanks, the players resurfaced every 30 seconds for air.

WOOL RUSH
In 40 hours, Garry Hebberman of Jamestown, Australia, sheared 1,054 sheep—that's one sheep every 2 minutes 17 seconds!

CROWDED WAVE
Timing things to perfection, 84 surfers simultaneously rode the same wave at Quebra Mar, Santos, Brazil, in 2007.

LET'S ROCK!
On January 27, 2007, Pat Callan of LaCrosse, Wisconsin, headbanged for more than 35 minutes straight at a rock concert.

HEADSTRONG
Appearing on a German TV show in 2007, Kevin Shelley of Carmel, Indiana, broke 46 wooden toilet seat lids in 60 seconds—with his head! It is not the first time he has used his head for entertainment—he has previously smashed ten pine boards with his head in just over seven seconds.

YOUNG SWIMMER
Leah Robbins of Norfolk, England, swam 164 ft (50 m) in May 2007—even though she was only two years old! She swam the distance backstroke, which is normally tackled by children three times her age.

SPEED-SKIPPER
Olga Berberich, a 23-year-old German fitness coach, completed 251 skips with a rope in one minute in Cologne in September 2007.

ROLLER-COASTER RIDE

Richard Rodriguez certainly experienced the ups and downs of life in 2007. The 48-year-old American roller-coaster enthusiast spent 17 consecutive days riding the Pepsi Max Big One at Blackpool Pleasure Beach in northern England.

He got a five-minute break every hour he was on the ride, and could save these up for longer breaks if he preferred. Eating, drinking, and sleeping on the roller coaster, Rodriguez completed nearly 8,000 rides and covered over 6,300 mi (10,140 km)—almost as far as the return journey from Blackpool to his hometown of Brooklyn, New York.

Ripley's ask

"When did you start riding roller coasters, and why? Initially, I was afraid of roller coasters and only rode my first white-knuckle coaster at the age of 16. As a child, Charles Lindbergh was my hero, and 1977 was the 50th anniversary of his solo nonstop flight across the Atlantic. He had previously ridden the Cyclone so, as a tribute to him, I did my first roller-coaster marathon.

Did you ever feel sick while on the Big One? I haven't been sick yet. The main thing that bothers me is the wind pressure against my skin. It's like sticking your head out of a car window for x amount of hours at 80 mph!

Did you get bored? Yes, but I find boredom less of an issue during the day because the general public can ride on the coaster with me. One little boy asked me if the park knew I was doing a roller-coaster marathon or was it a big secret!

Did you get a sore backside? I probably would—if I didn't sit on foam. I am quite particular about foam, it has to be a certain type (industrial packing foam) and cut to fit exactly (bottom size).

When you stepped off the roller coaster to have a break, did you feel unbalanced? I did get the odd wobble, yes. After a while it feels more normal to be on the roller coaster than on the ground.

Did you sleep on the roller coaster? Yes, but sporadically, and the first night is always very hard. However, I didn't sleep on the Big One, I slept on the nearby Big Dipper. The Big One isn't allowed to run at night because of noise pollution, so it was a quick change-over every evening.

Is there a particular roller coaster that you want to ride on? I'd like to do a coaster challenge in an exotic place like Japan or India."

Richard gets ready to bed down for the night on the Big Dipper surrounded by his protective foam padding.

The Big One rises majestically above the beach at Blackpool.

BUS RIDE

Bill Kazmaier of Burlington, Wisconsin, can pull a bus—full of schoolchildren! Three times crowned the world's strongest man, he can also lift a boy off the ground by means of a rope attached to just his little finger.

HELD BREATH

Freediver Dave Mullins from New Zealand swam 740 ft (226 m) in a Wellington swimming pool in 2007—on a single breath. He held his breath for 3 minutes 42 seconds.

PREVENTED TAKEOFF

In Superior, Minnesota, in 2007, Chad Netherland used his body strength to hold back two Cessna 206 airplanes from taking off in opposite directions for 60 seconds!

ROLL WITH IT

A toilet roll measuring more than 11 mi (18 km) long was unraveled at London's Wembley Stadium in July 2007. The toilet roll, which was 4 ft 10 in (1.5 m) wide and weighed 1,440 lb (653 kg), was almost as long as the Victoria Line in the English capital's subway system.

BIG CATCH

Over the past 25 years, fervent fisherman Dave Romeo of Mount Joy Township, Pennsylvania, has caught more than 25,000 bass! What's more, he keeps a journal detailing every bass he has ever hooked.

ONE FINGER

Ji Fengshan of Harbin city, China, can pull four taxis with just one finger! He has been building up the strength in the middle finger of his right hand for more than 40 years by using it to carry a bucket of water each day.

VERTICAL EGGS

To mark the summer solstice on June 21 in 2005, at 12 noon residents of Chiayi County, Taiwan, made 1,972 eggs stand on end simultaneously.

UP AND DOWN

Mark Anglesey of Yorkshire, England, lifted the back end of a car, weighing 450 lb (204 kg), at least 12 in (30 cm) off the ground 580 times in an hour.

STONE-SKIPPER

Russ Byars of Venango County, Pennsylvania, can skip a stone across water 51 times—reaching distances of up to 250 ft (76 m). He started stone-skipping eight years ago for something to do while out walking his dog. He favors smooth, rounded stones about 3–4 in (7–10 cm) across, grips them between his thumb and forefinger and, for maximum distance, adds spin and follow through.

PENNY LINE

In 2007, 80 penny-layers, mostly under the age of ten, set out 2,879 ft (878 m) of pennies in a parking lot at Hancock, Maine, in only 2 hours 26 minutes.

DIZZY HIPS

Many people can't run a mile in under eight minutes, but Paul Blair, aka Dizzy Hips, of San Francisco, California, can—and while twirling a hula hoop! He can also hula hoop while skating, skiing, or snow boarding and has performed a routine with a hula hoop measuring 43 ft (13 m) in circumference!

REVERSE GEAR

Germany's Isabella Wagner can complete the 100 meters running race in less than 17 seconds—while running backward!

SIMULATED KISS

A total of 3,249 residents of Taipei, Taiwan, simultaneously administered mouth-to-mouth resuscitation in September 2007. Ranging in age from a four-year-old girl to a 97-year-old grandmother, the volunteers gave simulated CPR (cardiopulmonary resuscitation) to plastic mannequins.

Hypnotic
POWER

Canadian hypnotist Ian Stewart is a firm believer in mind over matter. He shows the extreme power of the mind in a demonstration of self-hypnosis in which he endures the shock of more than 100 firecrackers taped to his chest going off with a bang!

TATTOO PARADE

In June 2005, people with tattooed backs paraded on the beach at Zandvoort, the Netherlands, forming a line measuring more than 3 mi (5 km) long.

GRAND REUNION

When Stadium High School at Tacoma, Washington, held its 100th anniversary reunion in 2007, no fewer than 3,299 former pupils showed up!

COLD FEET

Nico Surings, of Eindhoven, the Netherlands, braved the cold to run the 100 meters barefoot on ice, in 17.35 seconds in December 2006.

HUGE SLEEPOVER

Some 35,000 children from all over the U.K. staged a mass sleepover in June 2007. Nearly 1,000 different sleepovers occurred in schools and scout groups across the country.

TEA PARTY

Nearly 15,000 people took part in a mass tea party at Nishio, Aichi, Japan, in October 2006. Almost a mile of red carpet was used for the participants to sit or kneel on while they drank powdered green tea.

MARATHON DRIBBLE

In February 2006, Joseph Odhiambo, a 41-year-old schoolteacher from Phoenix, Arizona, dribbled a basketball through the streets of Houston, Texas, for a total of 26 hours 40 minutes. During that period he also managed to bounce the ball an estimated 140,000 times!

TOUGH GUY

York, Pennsylvania, strongman Chris Rider can perform amazing feats of strength. He can tear two car license plates in half simultaneously, break a baseball bat over his knee, bend an 8-in (20-cm) adjustable wrench, bend a metal horseshoe into the shape of a heart in just seven seconds, and break a 20-oz (567-g) hammer in two.

SNOW ANGELS

In February 2007 in Bismarck, North Dakota, 8,962 people waved their arms simultaneously while lying in the snow to create a multitude of snow angels.

CAN COLLECTION

Schools across South Africa collected nearly two million tin cans for recycling in just one month in 2007.

STITCH IN TIME

While running the 2007 London Marathon, 49-year-old Susie Hewer of Sussex, England, knitted a 4-ft-long (1.2-m) scarf! Susie, who describes herself as an "extreme knitter," still managed to complete the course in under six hours.

NOODLE KING!

From just 2 lb 3 oz (1 kg) of flour, Li Enhai, of China, can make more than 2,090,000 strings of noodles. The noodles he creates are so fine that 39 can pass through the eye of one needle!

HELICOPTER PULL
Lasha Pataraia pulled a 17,050-lb (7,734-kg) military helicopter for a staggering 86 ft 4 in (26.3 m) with only his ear at an airfield near Tbilisi, Georgia. One end of a rope was attached to his ear while the other was tied to the front wheel of the helicopter.

BOUNCE-JUGGLER
Tim Nolan of Virginia Beach, Virginia, can bounce-juggle 11 balls simultaneously. Bounce-juggling is the art of bouncing objects off the ground while juggling them.

BURSTING WITH PRIDE
John Cassidy of Philadelphia, Pennsylvania, created 747 balloon animals in one hour in 2007. His creations included dogs, turtles, snails, and fish. Afterward, he said his secret was "keep your cheeks in, blow hard, and think pure thoughts."

RECORD YEAR
Canadian singer/songwriter Kevin Bath recorded an album a week for an entire year—and with eight tracks per album, that came to 416 songs in 365 days. Working in his home studio, he adopted a strict schedule whereby he completed tracks on a Thursday and mixed them over the weekend for Sunday release. To save valuable time on shaving, he grew a beard for a while.

FLORAL RIBBON
To raise awareness for breast cancer, a Dubai healthcare group created a pink ribbon symbol measuring 95 ft (29 m) in length and made up of 105,000 carnations.

GIRL HERCULES
At age 13, Varya Akulova from Krivoy Rog, Ukraine, can lift 772 lb (350 kg)—nearly ten times her body weight. Known as "Girl Hercules," she is an accomplished arm wrestler and could carry three children on her shoulders at age ten.

HUGE GATHERING
A total of 3,500 priests took part in a single religious ceremony at Jaipur, India, in 2007. The ceremony, named Bhoomi Poojan, was held to worship a piece of land before it is put to use, and all of the participating priests dug the earth with pickaxes and hoes.

HAY RIDE
Organized by Bill Buckelew and an army of volunteers, a hay ride on a 500-ft-long (150-m) line of trucks and trailers carried 1,042 people at the 2007 Farm Day celebrations in DeFuniak Springs, Florida.

SUMO SQUATS
At the age of nearly 40, Dr. Thienna, a Vietnamese-born female fitness expert, performed 5,135 sumo squats in one hour in San Francisco, California, in December 2007.

STATESIDE RUN
In 2007, 36-year-old Reza Baluchi from Boulder, Colorado, spent six months running around the perimeter of the United States—a jog of over 11,000 mi (17,700 km). He started and finished in New York City, running an average of 55 mi (90 km) a day.

SHOW STOPPER

Instead of reaching for the off switch, Germany's Marco Boehm can stop a rotating electric fan with his tongue! He demonstrated his astounding art on a German TV show filmed in Mallorca, Spain, in June 2007.

FLAT OUT

With his legs split, chest bent forward, and chin almost skimming the ground, six-year-old Aniket Chindak of Belgaum, India, is so flexible that he can roller-skate under parked cars. Aniket is a leading exponent of the sport of limbo-skating and can also limbo under poles set just 8 in (20 cm) off the ground. Of his car-skating he says: "It took three months before I could get my body in the right position. The hardest thing is to go fast enough before I bend down, because that's how you can skate under the car and come out the other side."

Aniket shows off his incredible skill by limbo-skating under a car that sits just 9½ in (24 cm) off the ground.

Enter the Vault

LONG BEARD ▶

Edwin Smith, a miner in the California gold rush of the mid-1800s, liked his beard so much that he let it grow for 16 years. It reached a length of 8 ft (2.4 m) and was so long that Smith had to hire a servant just to wash and comb it.

▲ TREE HOUSE

This tree dwelling in Horatio, Arkansas, belonged to Fred Brown, who was known as the Human Owl. Nobody knew who he was nor where he came from, but he lived in the tree for more than ten years.

▼ HIGH-RISE FRED

In 1940, Chicagoan Fred Steinlauf, 18, could be seen riding through the streets of his hometown blindfolded on a 10-ft (3-m) unicycle.

DOGGONE CLEVER

Peppy, a Dalmatian owned by Bill Fontana of Fort Frances, Oregon, rolled a log lumberjack-style for a full mile in one hour in 1954.

▲ TREE MAN

For a period during the 1930s, "The Monkey Man" of Portsmouth, Rhode Island, spent all day every Sunday standing in a tree watching the cars go by.

PIANO MAN

Arthur Schultz of Hamtramck, Michigan, gave piano recitals in the 1930s, playing the instrument with the backs of his fingers.

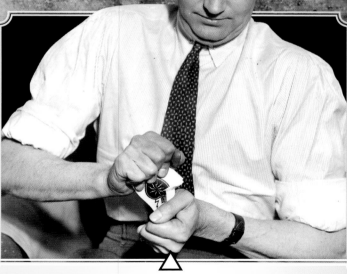

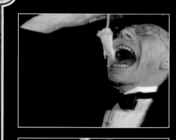

CUT THE DECK

In 1931, New Yorker W.M. Wright could perform the astonishing feat of tearing a regular deck of playing cards into eighths with his bare hands. The resulting pieces of card were no bigger than his thumbnails.

THE REGURGITATOR

In 1939, Dagmar Rothman performed at Ripley's New York City Odditorium astounding crowds by swallowing and regurgitating a live mouse. He smoked a cigarette before and during putting the mouse in his mouth, claiming that the smoke stunned the creature into lying still. Rothman could also place a whole lemon in his mouth.

ROLLER MAN

French designer Jean-Yves Blondeau can speed down a highway and even overtake motorbikes—just by wearing his "Buggy Rollin" suit. The plastic full-body suit has a set of rollers on most of the major joints, torso, and back, enabling him to roll along in any position at speeds of up to 60 mph (100 km/h).

MOBILE CATHEDRAL

Rebecca Caldwell of Oakland, California, has designed a car that looks like a Gothic cathedral, complete with flying buttresses, stained glass windows, and gargoyles. The framework of her "Carthedral" art car is a 1971 Cadillac hearse with a Volkswagen Beetle welded on top.

WHAT A CORKER!

Jan Elftmann of Minneapolis, Minnesota, has decorated her Mazda truck with more than 10,000 wine and champagne corks collected during her 13 years as a waitress in an Italian restaurant. To accompany the truck at art car parades, she wears a ball gown—also decorated with dozens of corks.

HEAVY METAL

A giant motorbike powered by a tank engine stands 17 ft 4 in (5.3 m) long, 7 ft 6 in (2.3 m) tall—and the engine alone weighs almost 2 tons. Dubbed the *Led Zeppelin* by its creator Tilo Nieber, the bike took a team of welders and mechanics from Zilly, Germany, almost a year to build.

CAREFUL DRIVER

A 94-year-old woman from Hereford, England, has driven over a period of 82 years more than 600,000 mi (965,600 km) without even the smallest accident. Muriel Gladwin, who taught herself to drive at age 12, has never even had a scrape—nor has she been booked for speeding.

IN THE GROOVE

Japanese engineers have created "Melody Roads" with specially cut grooves that develop pitched vibrations as a car drives over them.

GREEN MACHINE

Students at Warwick University, England, have created an eco-friendly sports car that has a body made from plants, and tires made from potatoes. Eco One uses pulped hemp injected with rapeseed oil for its bodywork, has brake pads constructed from ground cashew nuts, and runs on a fuel of fermented wheat and sugar beet. Even so, it can go from 0 to 60 mph (0 to 97 km/h) in 4 seconds and has a top speed of 150 mph (240 km/h).

BRICK TRUCK

Mark Monroe and students at Austin College, Sherman, Texas, created a station wagon that appears to be made of bricks. The Brickmobile is really a 1968 Ford Country Sedan with 839 brick-like ceramic tiles stuck to the bodywork.

MERCEDES BONZ

A Minnesota woman has spent four years covering a car in nearly 1,000 animal bones. B.J. Zander decorated her Mercedes Bonz—in reality a Volvo—with beef and chicken bones that she obtained from friends, butchers, and her dog.

WHEELCHAIR RACER

A German man was stopped by police for driving an electric wheelchair down the street at 40 mph (64 km/h)—twice the speed limit. Guenther Eichmann of Geseke had modified the wheelchair's engine so that it could go faster.

JET STOOL

If Tim Arfons fancies a quick drink, he climbs aboard his jet barstool. Powered by a gas turbine engine, the stool has reached speeds of 40 mph (64 km/h) at a raceway park in Norwalk, Ohio.

ELECTRIC TRICYCLE

To pull himself along while wearing rollerblades, Swiss figure skater Stephan Soder has designed an electric tricycle with a top speed of 12 mph (19 km/h). The Easyglider X6 has an electric-powered front wheel, a parking brake, a headlight, and three power levels. Optional extras include a music system.

PROPELLER CAR

Wanting a vehicle that he could take to both car and air shows, Dave Major of Benton, Kansas, designed the Aerocar, a cross between a little 1959 BMW 600 and an airplane. The roadworthy auto has a handmade propeller turned by an electric motor, a tail from a real airplane, and tires from a jet. Even though it never leaves the ground, it has a custom dash with a working altimeter and an airspeed indicator.

MECHANICAL SPIDER

Designers from Vancouver, British Columbia, Canada, have created a huge mechanical spider that a person can ride. Powered by a Honda engine and a system of hydraulic pumps and motors, the Mondo Spider is an eight-legged mechanical walking machine that stands 5 ft (1.5 m) high and 8 ft (2.4 m) wide with a seat at the front. The steel legs move like a spider and give it a top speed of 4 ft (1.2 m) per second, which is the equivalent of a brisk human walk.

GRASS COVERING

Ephraim Eusebio, of Minneapolis, Minnesota, drives a 1991 Toyota Previa that is covered in artificial grass salvaged from the Guthrie Theater's garbage.

LUGE RACER

Lying horizontally just a couple of inches above the asphalt, Joel King of Sussex, England, reached a speed of 112 mph (180 km/h) on a jet-powered street luge board in August 2007. He says that stopping is the hardest part. "When you've finished you turn the engine off and use your feet to brake, which at over 100 mph is quite interesting."

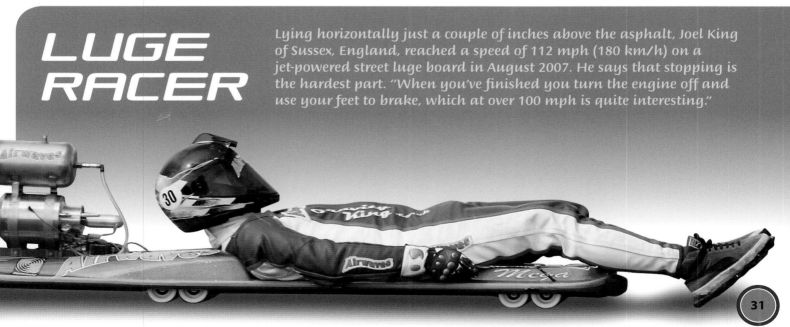

JUNIOR COWBOY

Max Mobley of Kennett, Missouri, is one of the country's leading practitioners of Wild West arts—and he's only eight years old! Yet Max is no newcomer to his unusual hobby—he has been cracking and spinning ropes since he could walk.

MIGHTY ATOM

He stood only 54 in (137 cm) tall, but David Moyer of Reading, Pennsylvania, won 23 national titles in weight lifting, held national and world records, and could bench press more than twice his own weight.

SIMON SAYS

A total of 1,100 freshmen from the University of Miami gathered at the city's Bank United Center in August 2007 and simultaneously played the mimicking game "Simon Says."

KEEN TYPIST

Les Stewart of Mudjimba, Australia, spent 15 years typing out all the numbers from one to one million in letters, simply because he "wanted something to do." Between 1983 and 1998 he typed for 20 minutes every waking hour—on the hour—eventually filling 19,890 pages. Once he had finished, he threw all the pages out, except for the first and the last sheets. Stewart is no stranger to odd feats—he once put 3,400 stamps on a single envelope.

WIDE AWAKE

Tony Wright from Penzance, Cornwall, England, stayed awake for an incredible 11 days and nights in May 2007—a total of 266 hours. He prepared for the challenge by eating a diet of raw vegetables, fruit, nuts, and seeds, which, he says, helped his brain to stay awake and remain functional for long periods of time. He also fought off waves of tiredness by drinking tea, playing pool, and keeping a diary.

TEEN TEXTER

A 13-year-old girl who sends an average of 8,000 texts a month was crowned U.S. texting champion in 2007. Morgan Pozgar of Claysburg, Pennsylvania, beat off competition from 300 rivals to land the title in New York. She was not short of practice—she sends about 260 texts a day (roughly one every five minutes) to her friends.

CAR PUSH

In September 2006, Rob Kmet and Teri Starr of Winnipeg, Manitoba, Canada, pushed a Dodge Neon more than 50 mi (80 km) around a racetrack over a period of 21 hours. They trained for the event by lifting weights and jogging in the shallow water of a lake.

WEIGHT LOSS

In just one year, 42-year-old Manuel Uribe of Monterrey, Mexico, shed 440 lb (200 kg)! In early 2006 he weighed a colossal 1,235 lb (560 kg)—over half a ton—but within 12 months his low-carb diet had taken him almost halfway to achieving his ultimate goal of losing 1,000 lb (454 kg).

LONG LINE DANCE

In August 2007, more than 17,000 dancers formed an enormous line dance at the Ebony Black Family Reunion Tour in Atlanta, Georgia.

PRETTY PRANK

Walt, a prank-loving employee at a company in Washington, D.C., returned to the parking garage one day to find his beloved Jaguar car covered in 14,000 multi-colored sticky notes! Every inch of the car—including the tires—was covered except for the hood ornament and license plate. It had taken co-worker Scott Ableman and a dozen colleagues less than two hours to pull off the elaborate joke. Luckily, Walt saw the funny side and, once he'd cleaned off the windshield, drove the car home to show his family.

RUN OVER
Patrick Chege of Kenya, allows heavy trucks to run over his chest and gets up afterward without injury!

ON-AIR MILES
U.S. TV host Jimmy Kimmel commuted 22,406 mi (36,060 km) during one week in October 2007. He filled in every day for Regis Philbin on *Live with Regis & Kelly* in New York City and then jumped on a plane to host his late-night talk show in Los Angeles.

WOBBLE BOARDS
A total of 487 students, teachers, and adults at Eisenhower Junior High School in Taylorsville, Utah, gathered in November 2007 to form a huge wobble board ensemble. Popularized by the Australian entertainer Rolf Harris, wobble boards are musical instruments made of hardboards measuring 2 x 3 ft (60 x 90 cm). They are played by propping them between the palms of the hands and bouncing them back and forth.

BEER CARRYING
In 2007, Reinhard Wurz of Australia, carried 20 one-liter (32-fl oz) glasses full of beer for a distance of 130 ft (40 m).

SMASH HIT
Dan Wilson from Lodi, California, smashed 64 dinner plates on his forehead in 41 seconds in 2007. The 47-year-old father-of-eight, who also breaks bottles, bricks, and boards on his head, said of his achievement: "I wanted to do something famous before I die and as I don't have the brains, I thought I'd better use my body." He added that he spends about two hours psyching himself up before each challenge, concentrating all his energy on one quarter-sized spot at the top of his forehead.

DOMINO TOPPLING
A TV commercial filmed in Salta, Argentina, in 2007 featured 6,000 dominoes toppling in just 14 seconds. The domino trail took two days to construct and also involved 10,000 books, 400 tires, 45 dressers, and six cars.

CHECKMATE K.O.
In November 2007, German policeman Frank Stoldt was crowned world champion of the hybrid sport of chessboxing. Bouts are composed of up to 11 alternating rounds of chess and boxing, representing the ultimate test of brains and brawn. After fending off his American opponent's punches, Stoldt managed to clinch the title with a checkmate in the chess game of the seventh round.

MASS DRIBBLE
Led by the Indiana Pacers basketball team, around 4,600 people dribbled basketballs through Indianapolis in October 2007.

WORM DANCE
James Rubec performed a "Worm" break dance move along the turf of the Rogers Centre stadium in Toronto, Ontario, Canada, for more than 98 ft (30 m) in 2007.

BLINDFOLDED TEXT
New Zealand teenager Elliot Nicholls sent a 160-character text message in just 45 seconds... while blindfolded. The 17-year-old sends around 50 text messages a day and has worn out the keypads on four cell phones already.

GORILLA SUIT
Ferrari Formula One driver Kimi Raikkonen entered a powerboat race in the Finnish city of Hanko in July 2007 wearing a gorilla suit to disguise his identity.

ALL SCORED
Every soccer player in a 12-man squad scored when Bridlington Rangers Blues Under-13s beat Hutton Cranswick United 23–0 in a match in Yorkshire, England, in 2007. As the boys switched positions, even the goalkeeper scored three times.

TWISTER GAME
More than 1,400 people played a mass game of Twister at the Rogers Centre Stadium in Toronto, Ontario, Canada, in 2007.

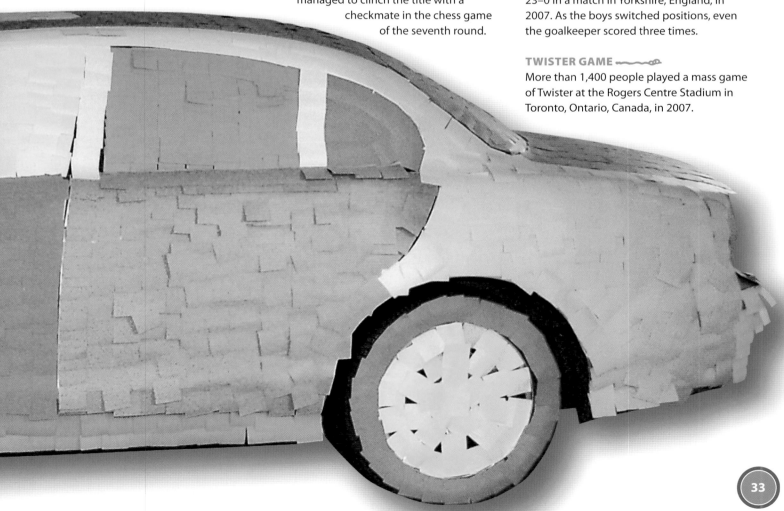

Index

Page numbers in *italics* refer to illustrations

ACKNOWLEDGMENTS

COVER (l) Tim Arfons, (t/r) Scott Ableman, (b/r) www.darsshoeheaven.com/www.justtherightshoeheavenworldwide.com; BACK COVER Joel King/Wrigley's Airwaves ®; 4 Tim Arfons; 6–7 www.carlwarner.com; 8 UPPA/Photoshot; 9 (t) CNImaging/Photoshot, (b) UPPA/Photoshot; 10 (b/c, b/r) Brad Meyer, (r) Dusty Bastian; 11 (t) Reuters/Claro Cortes; 12–13 Jin Siliu/ChinaFotoPress/Photocome/PA Photos; 13 ChinaFotoPress/Photocome/PA Photos; 14–15 www.darsshoeheaven.com/www.justtherightshoeheavenworldwide.com; 16–17 Hermann J. Knippertz/AP/PA Photos; 18 ChinaFotoPress/Photocome/PA Photos; 19 AFP/Getty Images; 20–21 ©Veniamin's Human Slinky Author; Ioan ®Veniamin Oprea President of ®Veniamin Shows, Inc.; 22 (bgd, b) Courtesy of Pleasure Beach, Blackpool, (t) Martin Rickett/PA Wire/PA Photos; 23 Phil Mesibar www.mesibar.com/Paul Blair www.DizzyHips.com; 24 Babineau Photography; 25 (t/l, t/c) ChinaFotoPress/Photocome/PA Photos, (b) Reuters/POOL New; 26–27 Simon de Trey-White/Barcroft Media; 30 ChinaFotoPress/Cheng Jiang/Photocome/PA Photos; 31 (t) Tim Arfons, (b) Joel King/Wrigley's Airwaves®; 32–33 Scott Ableman

Key: t = top, b = bottom, c = center, l = left, r = right, sp = single page, dp = double page

All other photos are from Ripley Entertainment Inc.
Every attempt has been made to acknowledge correctly and contact copyright holders and we apologize in advance for any unintentional errors or omissions, which will be corrected in future editions.